The Dark Prince

Andrew Lancaster and The Olympians, Volume 3

Tharun Vigneswar PS

Published by Tharun Vigneswar PS, 2024.

THE DARK PRINCE

First edition. August 15, 2024.

ISBN: 979-8227311528

Written by Tharun Vigneswar PS.

Chapter 1

THE IMMORTAL ALLIANCE

In the depths of Tartarus, where darkness reigned supreme and the air crackled with ancient power, Andrew, Kiara, Harry, and Adrian stood together, their souls weighed down by the burden of their banishment from Olympus. As they navigated the twisting corridors of the abyss, a sense of foreboding hung heavy in the air, each step bringing them closer to their fateful encounter.

Suddenly, from the shadows emerged Tartarus himself, a towering figure cloaked in darkness and surrounded by an aura of primal energy. His eyes, deep pools of shadow, seemed to pierce through their very souls as he regarded them with a mixture of curiosity and amusement.

"Welcome, children of Olympus," Tartarus boomed, his voice echoing off the cavern walls. "I have been expecting you."

Andrew, his gaze steady and unwavering, met Tartarus's gaze head-on. "We seek power," he declared, his voice tinged with defiance. "Power to challenge the gods who have cast us aside. Power to claim what is rightfully ours."

Tartarus chuckled, the sound like the rumble of distant thunder. "Ah, I see," he said, his voice dripping with amusement. "You seek to challenge the gods, do you? A bold ambition, indeed."

"But not an impossible one," Kiara interjected, her voice firm and resolute. "We are prepared to do whatever it takes to reclaim our rightful place among the Olympians."

Tartarus regarded them for a moment, his expression inscrutable. Then, with a gesture of his hand, he summoned forth an army of shadows and twisted creatures, their forms shifting and writhing in the darkness.

"You are not alone in your desire for vengeance," Tartarus said, his voice resonating with power. "I, too, seek to overthrow the gods and claim dominion over Olympus. And according to the ancient prophecies, it is you, Andrew, who shall lead us to victory."

Andrew's eyes widened in surprise, his mind racing with the implications of Tartarus's words. Could it be true? Was he truly destined to lead an army against the gods themselves?

With a solemn nod, Andrew stepped forward, his resolve hardening with each passing moment. "Then let us forge an alliance," he declared, his voice ringing with conviction. "An alliance born of our shared desire for freedom and justice. An alliance that will shake the very foundations of Olympus."

And so, beneath the watchful gaze of Tartarus, the Immortal Alliance was formed, its members bound together by their shared ambition and determination to challenge the might of the gods. As they clasped hands in solidarity, their fate was sealed.

With a nod of agreement, Tartarus led Andrew deeper into the labyrinthine depths of Tartarus, the darkness closing in around them like a suffocating shroud. Each step felt heavier than the last, as if the weight of their shared destiny bore down upon them with relentless force.

Finally, they reached the heart of the abyss, where the very fabric of reality seemed to fray and unravel. Here, in the deepest recesses of Tartarus, lay the domain of Chaos, the primordial force of creation and destruction.

As they approached, the air crackled with raw energy, sending shivers down Andrew's spine. He could feel the power of Chaos coursing through the very fabric of existence, a force beyond comprehension and control.

Tartarus bowed low before the swirling vortex of darkness that marked the entrance to Chaos's domain, his voice reverent as he addressed the primordial deity.

"Chaos, ruler of the void, we seek an audience with you," Tartarus intoned, his words echoing through the endless expanse of the abyss.

For a moment, there was silence, broken only by the distant rumble of cosmic energy. Then, from the heart of the swirling vortex, a voice spoke, its tone ancient and timeless.

"Who dares disturb my slumber?" it demanded, its words resonating with power.

"It is I, Tartarus, lord of the abyss, and I bring with me Andrew, chosen champion of the Immortal Alliance," Tartarus replied, his voice unwavering.

Andrew stepped forward, his heart pounding in his chest as he gazed into the swirling depths of Chaos's domain. He knew that this moment would shape the course of his destiny, that he stood on the threshold of power beyond imagining.

"Chaos," he began, his voice steady despite the tremors of uncertainty that gripped him. "We seek your aid in our quest to overthrow the gods and claim dominion over Olympus. Will you stand with us in our hour of need?"

There was a moment of tense silence, as if the very fabric of reality held its breath in anticipation. Then, with a deafening roar, the vortex of darkness parted, revealing the form of Chaos herself.

She was a swirling mass of cosmic energy, her form shifting and changing with each passing moment. Her eyes, twin orbs of swirling chaos, regarded Andrew with a mixture of curiosity and amusement.

"So, you seek to challenge the gods," she mused, her voice echoing through the abyss. "A bold ambition, indeed. But know this, champion of the Immortal Alliance: the path you tread is fraught with danger and uncertainty. Are you prepared to face the consequences of your actions?"

Andrew met Chaos's gaze head-on, his resolve unwavering. "I am," he declared, his voice ringing with conviction. "For the sake of freedom and justice, I will do whatever it takes to claim what is rightfully ours."

Chaos regarded him for a moment, her eyes shining with an otherworldly light. Then, with a nod of approval, she extended a hand towards Andrew, her form shimmering with cosmic energy.

"Very well, chosen champion of the Immortal Alliance," she said, her voice carrying the weight of the cosmos itself. "I shall lend you my aid in your quest for vengeance. Together, we shall shake the very foundations of Olympus and usher in a new era of darkness."

And with that, Andrew grasped Chaos's hand, his destiny intertwined with the primordial force of creation and destruction. As they stood together on the threshold of chaos and possibility, the stage was set for a conflict that would shape the fate of the cosmos itself.

With Chaos's proclamation, the very fabric of reality seemed to shift, as if acknowledging Andrew's newfound status as her chosen heir. Tartarus, once the imposing lord of the abyss, now bowed low before Andrew, his allegiance sworn to the champion of the Immortal Alliance.

"As Chaos's heir, your will shall be law," Tartarus declared, his voice reverberating through the abyss. "I pledge my loyalty to you, Andrew, and shall serve you faithfully in the coming conflict."

Andrew felt a surge of power coursing through him, the weight of his newfound authority settling upon his shoulders like a mantle of darkness. He knew that with Chaos's support, they stood on the brink of greatness, ready to challenge the gods themselves for control of Olympus.

But even as he embraced his new role, Andrew could not shake the sense of unease that gnawed at the edges of his consciousness. He knew that the path ahead would be fraught with peril, and that the choices he made would shape the destiny of the cosmos itself.

"We shall not falter in our quest," Andrew declared, his voice resonating with determination. "Together, we shall overthrow the gods and claim what is rightfully ours. Let Olympus tremble before the might of the Immortal Alliance!"

With his allies at his side and the power of Chaos coursing through his veins, Andrew knew that they were ready to face whatever challenges lay ahead. The stage was set for a conflict unlike any the world had ever seen, and he was determined to emerge victorious, no matter the cost.

With the weight of Chaos's authority behind him, Andrew felt a newfound sense of purpose coursing through his veins. He turned to his companions, Kiara, Harry, and Adrian, their faces illuminated by the dim glow of the abyss.

"We have the support of Chaos herself," Andrew declared, his voice tinged with a mix of awe and determination. "With her backing, there is nothing we cannot achieve."

Kiara nodded in agreement, her eyes blazing with determination. "Together, we shall forge an army the likes of which

Olympus has never seen," she proclaimed, her voice echoing through the darkness.

Harry and Adrian exchanged a knowing glance, their resolve unyielding in the face of the challenges ahead. "The gods will rue the day they banished us," Harry declared, his voice tinged with a hint of defiance.

Adrian nodded in agreement, his hands clenched into fists at his sides. "We shall show them the true meaning of power," he vowed, his voice carrying an undercurrent of determination.

With their resolve steeled and their purpose clear, the four companions set about the task of building their army. Tartarus, ever loyal to Andrew as Chaos's chosen heir, pledged the support of the denizens of the abyss, promising to rally them to their cause.

And so, with the Immortal Alliance forged and their sights set on Olympus, Andrew and his companions set out to challenge the gods themselves, ready to seize their rightful place as rulers of the cosmos. They were determined to emerge victorious, no matter the cost.

Chapter 2

THE ALLIANCE OF SHADOWS

Their path led them to a grand, cavernous chamber at the heart of Tartarus's domain. Here, the very air seemed thick with primordial energy, and the shadows danced with a life of their own. Tartarus, Nyx, and Chaos awaited them, their presences a potent reminder of the ancient forces they had allied with.

"Welcome to the heart of the abyss," Tartarus intoned, his voice echoing with a gravity that matched the weight of the moment. "It is here that we shall seal our alliance, binding our fates together through ritual and ceremony."

Nyx, the goddess of night, stepped forward, her form shrouded in darkness that seemed to swallow the light. "The bond we forge today will be one of power and necessity," she said, her voice a soft whisper that carried across the chamber. "The rituals we perform will imbue you with the strength and abilities needed to challenge the gods themselves."

Chaos, an ever-shifting vortex of energy, hovered nearby, her voice resonating with both creation and destruction. "Prepare yourselves," she warned. "The path we tread is fraught with danger and uncertainty, but through unity and determination, we shall prevail."

The rituals began with a solemn procession to the altar of obsidian at the chamber's center. Each step felt like a journey through the annals of time, a walk through the shadows of history and destiny. The air crackled with raw energy, and the walls seemed to pulse with the heartbeat of the abyss.

Andrew stood before the altar, his heart racing. Tartarus approached him, a dagger of dark stone in hand. "This blade, forged in the depths of the abyss, will mark you with the symbols of power," Tartarus explained. He raised the dagger and etched a series of intricate symbols into Andrew's skin. Each cut burned with an otherworldly fire, but Andrew endured the pain, knowing that these marks were the key to their future.

Next, Nyx approached, her touch as cold as the void. She anointed Andrew with the essence of night, a thick, inky substance that seeped into his very being. "The night shall cloak you, protect you, and grant you strength," she whispered, her words weaving through the air like a dark melody.

Finally, Chaos extended a hand, her form a swirling maelstrom of energy. As Andrew grasped her hand, he felt a surge of power unlike anything he had ever experienced. "You are now my heir," Chaos declared, her voice echoing through his mind. "Wield my power wisely and reshape the cosmos as you see fit."

One by one, Kiara, Harry, and Adrian underwent the same rituals. Each was marked by Tartarus, anointed by Nyx, and infused with Chaos's energy. As the ceremonies concluded, the chamber hummed with the combined power of the abyss, night, and chaos. The Immortal Alliance had been irrevocably transformed, their bodies and souls bound to the ancient forces that would guide them in their quest.

With the rituals complete, Andrew and his companions turned their focus to mastering their newfound abilities. Each of them was paired with one of their ancient allies, who would serve as their mentor and guide.

Andrew's training began under the stern eye of Tartarus. The lord of the abyss taught him to harness the shadows, to command them with a thought and shape them to his will. In the vast, echoing caverns of Tartarus's domain, Andrew practiced summoning darkness to cloak himself, creating weapons from the shadows, and using the abyssal energy to enhance his physical strength.

"Feel the shadows as an extension of yourself," Tartarus instructed. "They are not mere tools but a part of your very essence. Master them, and you shall command the power of the abyss."

Kiara's training was under the watchful guidance of Nyx. The goddess of night taught her to manipulate the darkness, to become one with the night. Kiara learned to blend into the shadows, rendering herself invisible to both mortal and divine eyes. She practiced creating fields of impenetrable darkness to disorient and confuse her enemies, and drawing strength from the night to enhance her speed and agility.

"The night is your ally, Kiara," Nyx explained. "Embrace its mysteries, and you shall find power beyond measure."

Harry and Adrian trained together with Chaos. The primordial force of creation and destruction demanded both strength and adaptability. Harry focused on channeling Chaos's destructive energy, creating blasts of raw power that could devastate anything in their path. He also learned to enhance his physical abilities, becoming a juggernaut of chaos.

Adrian, meanwhile, explored the creative aspect of Chaos's power. He learned to manipulate the raw energy into complex constructs, forging weapons and defenses from the very essence of creation. Chaos pushed them to think beyond conventional limits, encouraging them to embrace the unpredictable nature of her power.

"Chaos is the essence of possibility," Chaos explained. "To master it, you must be willing to embrace both order and disorder, creation and destruction."

As they trained, the Immortal Alliance also worked to integrate their abilities, developing tactics and strategies that would allow them to function as a cohesive unit. They practiced coordinated maneuvers, combining their powers to create devastating effects. Andrew's command of shadows allowed him to scout and ambush, while Kiara's manipulation of night provided cover and confusion. Harry's raw power and Adrian's constructs created a formidable offense and defense.

Their training sessions were grueling, but each day they grew stronger, more adept at wielding their powers. The bond between them deepened as they pushed each other to new heights, driven by their shared goal of overthrowing the gods.

With their abilities honed, the Immortal Alliance turned their attention to the strategic aspects of their impending war against Olympus. They knew that brute force alone would not be enough to topple the gods; they needed to outthink and outmaneuver their enemies.

The grand hall of their stronghold in Tartarus became a war room, filled with maps, charts, and magical artifacts. Tartarus, Nyx, and Chaos joined the strategy sessions, lending their ancient wisdom and experience to the planning process.

"We must understand our enemy," Andrew began, addressing the assembled group. "The gods are powerful, but they are not infallible. We need to identify their weaknesses and exploit them."

Kiara suggested, "We need intelligence on their movements and defenses. We should send scouts to gather information and identify key targets."

Harry added, "We should consider forming alliances with other beings who oppose the gods. There are many who have been wronged by Olympus and would join our cause."

Adrian emphasized, "We must prepare for counterattacks. The gods will not sit idly by while we gather our forces. We need to fortify our stronghold and be ready to defend it."

Tartarus, Nyx, and Chaos each contributed their insights. Tartarus stressed the importance of understanding the terrain and using the natural advantages of their domain. Nyx suggested using the cover of night for surprise attacks and ambushes. Chaos advocated for unconventional tactics, leveraging their unique powers to create confusion and disruption among the gods.

Together, they developed a comprehensive strategy that included reconnaissance, recruitment, and preparation for both offensive and defensive operations. They identified key targets within Olympus, such as important temples, supply lines, and key gods who posed significant threats. They also planned a series of feints and diversions to keep the gods off balance and prevent them from mounting a coordinated defense.

As they refined their plans, the Immortal Alliance also focused on fortifying their stronghold in Tartarus. They constructed defenses, set traps, and created fallback positions to ensure they could withstand any attacks from the gods. Adrian's constructs played a key role in these efforts, creating barriers and fortifications that were both sturdy and adaptable.

The Immortal Alliance was not alone in their struggle. As their preparations continued, they were approached by unexpected allies who shared their disdain for the gods and their desire for change.

One day, as the alliance was deep in discussion, a figure emerged from the shadows, his presence both commanding and serene. It was

Chiron, the wise centaur and renowned trainer of heroes. Behind him stood a group of demigods from Camp Half-Blood, their faces a mix of determination and hope.

"I have heard of your cause," Chiron said, his voice calm and steady. "Many of my former students have suffered under the tyranny of Olympus. I offer my knowledge and skills, and the support of Camp Half-Blood, to aid you in your quest."

Andrew stepped forward to greet Chiron, recognizing the centaur's legendary reputation. "Your presence and wisdom will be invaluable to us," he said, extending a hand. "We are honored to have you and your camp join our alliance."

Chiron nodded, a hint of a smile on his lips. "Together, we shall forge a path to victory."

Jason, a demigod with a commanding presence, stepped forward from the group. "We have fought the gods' battles long enough," he declared. "It is time we take a stand for our own freedom. Camp Half-Blood stands with you."

The demigods of Camp Half-Blood were a welcome addition to the alliance. Their combat skills, honed through years of training, and their diverse abilities, derived from their divine parentage, added a new layer of strength to the Immortal Alliance.

Andrew addressed the newcomers, his voice filled with conviction. "With Chiron's wisdom and the strength of Camp Half-Blood, our alliance grows stronger. We are united by a common goal, and together, we shall bring the gods to their knees."

With their alliances solidified, their powers honed, and their strategies developed, the Immortal Alliance stood on the brink of war. They had transformed from a group of banished immortals into a formidable force, united in their quest to overthrow the gods and claim dominion over the cosmos. As they prepared to take their first steps towards Olympus, they knew that their journey would be long and fraught with peril. But they were ready, and they were determined to succeed.

The darkness of Tartarus seemed to pulse with anticipation, as if the very realm itself was eager to see the outcome of their struggle. Andrew, now bearing the mantle of Chaos's chosen heir, felt the weight of their shared destiny pressing upon him. With his allies by his side and the power of the ancient forces behind him, he was ready to lead the Immortal Alliance into battle and reclaim their rightful place among the gods.

Chapter 3

THE GATHERING STORM

their power solidified with the support of Chaos, Tartarus, and Nyx. With the addition of Chiron and the demigods of Camp Half-Blood, the Immortal Alliance was ready to expand their reach and recruit more allies from various realms. The next steps in their grand plan required journeys to the farthest reaches of the underworld and beyond, seeking the aid of powerful entities and spirits who harbored their own grievances against Olympus.

Their first destination was Erebus, the shadowy realm between the living world and the Underworld, where the spirits of the dead roamed. Erebus was a place of perpetual twilight, its landscape a haunting mixture of desolate plains and spectral forests. It was here that the spirits of the dead lingered, waiting for their eventual journey to the Underworld.

Andrew, Kiara, Harry, Adrian, and a select group of demigods from Camp Half-Blood prepared for the journey. Chiron, with his vast knowledge of the ancient realms, provided guidance and wisdom for the perilous mission.

"Remember," Chiron cautioned as they prepared to depart, "Erebus is a realm of shadows and echoes. The spirits you encounter may be restless and vengeful. Approach them with respect and understanding."

The journey to Erebus began with a descent into a hidden cavern deep within Tartarus, where a portal to the shadowy realm awaited. The air grew colder and the light dimmer as they approached the portal, a swirling vortex of darkness that pulsed with an eerie, otherworldly energy.

As they stepped through the portal, the landscape of Erebus unfolded before them. The sky was a perpetual twilight, neither day nor night, and the ground was covered in a thick mist that seemed to swallow sound. Shadows flitted at the edges of their vision, and the air was filled with the faint whispers of the departed.

Andrew led the way, his senses heightened by the presence of Chaos's power within him. He could feel the restless energy of the spirits, their voices a cacophony of sorrow and anger. They needed to find a way to communicate with the spirits, to convince them to join their cause.

Kiara, with her affinity for the night, stepped forward. She closed her eyes and extended her senses, reaching out to the spirits with a soothing, calming presence. "We come in peace," she whispered, her voice carrying through the mist like a gentle breeze. "We seek your aid in our struggle against the gods of Olympus."

The whispers grew louder, and the shadows began to coalesce into forms. Ghostly figures emerged from the mist, their eyes glowing with an ethereal light. One spirit, an ancient warrior with a spectral sword at his side, stepped forward.

"Why should we aid you?" the warrior demanded, his voice echoing with the weight of centuries. "We are the forgotten, the forsaken. What do you offer us in return?"

Andrew stepped forward, his eyes meeting the warrior's. "We offer you a chance for justice," he said, his voice steady and resolute. "The gods of Olympus have wronged us all. Join us, and together we can overthrow their tyranny and bring about a new order."

The warrior regarded Andrew for a long moment, his expression unreadable. Then, with a nod, he turned to the other spirits. "I have seen the truth in his words," he declared. "We shall join the Immortal Alliance and fight for our freedom."

With the spirits of Erebus now allied with them, the Immortal Alliance's ranks swelled with new strength. The spirits, though ethereal, possessed a fierce determination and a deep-seated desire for vengeance that matched their own.

The next step in their journey took them deeper into the Underworld, to the very domain of Hades himself. Hades, the god of the Underworld, held sway over the dead and the subterranean realms. His support would be invaluable in their struggle against Olympus, but securing it would not be easy.

Chiron, once again, provided guidance as they prepared for the diplomatic mission. "Hades is a complex figure," he explained. "He is not easily swayed by promises or threats. You must appeal to his sense of justice and his desire to maintain balance in the cosmos."

The journey to the Underworld began at the River Styx, the boundary between the world of the living and the realm of the dead. They were ferried across the river by Charon, the grim boatman, who eyed them with suspicion but said nothing.

As they disembarked on the shores of the Underworld, the landscape was both awe-inspiring and terrifying. The sky was a deep, oppressive gray, and the ground was covered in jagged rocks and sulfurous fumes. The air was heavy with the weight of countless souls, and the cries of the damned echoed in the distance.

Andrew led the way, his resolve unwavering. They were escorted by a contingent of Hades' skeletal guards, their hollow eyes watching every move. The path to Hades' palace was lined with statues of the dead, their faces frozen in expressions of despair.

At last, they arrived at the grand, foreboding gates of Hades' palace. The gates creaked open, revealing the imposing figure of

Hades himself, seated upon a throne of obsidian and bone. His eyes, dark as the abyss, regarded them with a mixture of curiosity and suspicion.

"Why do you come before me, Andrew, heir of Chaos?" Hades' voice was cold and commanding. "What do you seek in my realm?"

Andrew stepped forward, his gaze steady. "We seek your support in our struggle against Olympus," he declared. "The gods have wronged us all, and their tyranny must end. Join us, and together we can reshape the cosmos."

Hades leaned back on his throne, his expression thoughtful. "You speak of rebellion and change," he mused. "But what guarantee do I have that your cause will succeed? The gods are powerful and vengeful."

Kiara stepped forward, her voice calm and persuasive. "We do not ask for blind allegiance," she said. "We ask for an alliance based on mutual benefit. The gods have shown their disregard for the balance of the cosmos. With your support, we can restore that balance and ensure justice for all."

Hades regarded them in silence for a long moment. Then, with a nod, he rose from his throne. "Very well," he declared. "I shall lend my support to your cause. But know this: the path you tread is fraught with peril, and the consequences of failure will be dire."

With Hades' support secured, the Immortal Alliance gained a powerful new ally. The forces of the Underworld, commanded by the god of the dead himself, would bolster their strength and provide invaluable resources in their struggle against Olympus.

With their new alliances in place, the Immortal Alliance faced one final challenge: proving their worthiness to their new allies. Both the spirits of Erebus and the forces of the Underworld demanded that they undergo trials to demonstrate their strength, resolve, and commitment to their cause.

The trials were held in a vast, ancient arena deep within the Underworld. The arena was a place of legend, where heroes and gods had tested their mettle against the most formidable challenges. The ground was stained with the blood of countless battles, and the air was thick with the scent of sweat and fear.

The first trial was a test of strength. Andrew, Harry, and a group of demigods faced off against a series of powerful adversaries, including monstrous beasts and skilled warriors. The battles were fierce and unrelenting, but Andrew's command of shadows and Harry's raw power proved decisive. They fought with determination and skill, emerging victorious and earning the respect of their allies.

The second trial was a test of cunning. Kiara and Adrian were tasked with navigating a labyrinth filled with traps and illusions, designed to confound and disorient. Kiara's affinity for the night allowed her to see through the darkness, while Adrian's constructs provided protection and guidance. Together, they outsmarted the labyrinth's challenges and reached the center, demonstrating their ingenuity and resourcefulness.

The final trial was a test of resolve. The entire Immortal Alliance faced a vision of their deepest fears and doubts, conjured by the spirits of Erebus. They were confronted with visions of failure, betrayal, and loss, designed to break their spirit and sow discord. But Andrew, drawing on the strength of Chaos and the support of his companions, led them through the trial with unwavering determination. They faced their fears head-on and emerged stronger, their bond unbreakable.

With the trials complete, the spirits of Erebus and the forces of the Underworld acknowledged the worthiness of the Immortal

Alliance. Their loyalty was now secured, and their commitment to the cause unwavering.

With their alliances solidified and their worthiness proven, the Immortal Alliance turned their focus to preparing for the impending war against Olympus. They established a war council, composed of representatives from each of their allies, to coordinate their efforts and plan their strategy.

The council met in the grand hall of Tartarus, where a massive map of the cosmos lay spread before them. Tartarus, Nyx, and Chaos took their places at the head of the table, alongside Andrew, Kiara, Harry, Adrian, and Chiron. Representatives from the spirits of Erebus, the forces of the Underworld, and Camp Half-Blood also took their seats, their faces set with determination.

"We have gathered formidable allies," Andrew began, addressing the council. "But the gods of Olympus are powerful and cunning. We must strike with precision and unity, leveraging our unique strengths to achieve victory."

The council debated their strategy, considering various approaches and tactics. They identified key targets within Olympus, including Zeus, Poseidon, and Hera, and developed plans to neutralize their power and influence. They also discussed ways to exploit the weaknesses of the gods, using their arrogance and overconfidence against them.

Kiara proposed a series of coordinated strikes, designed to sow confusion and discord among the gods. "We must strike swiftly and decisively," she argued. "By attacking multiple targets simultaneously, we can stretch their defenses thin and create opportunities for our forces to gain the upper hand."

Harry and Adrian suggested leveraging their newfound allies' unique abilities. "The spirits of Erebus can disrupt the gods' communications and sow fear among their ranks," Harry proposed. "Meanwhile, the forces of the Underworld can launch surprise attacks from below, striking at the heart of Olympus when they least expect it."

Chiron, with his vast knowledge of ancient strategies and tactics, provided invaluable insights. "We must also be prepared for the gods' retaliation," he cautioned. "They will not take our challenge lightly. We must fortify our positions and ensure our allies are ready for the inevitable counterattacks."

As the council finalized their plans, Andrew felt a sense of anticipation and resolve. The time for preparation was drawing to a close, and the moment of reckoning was fast approaching. With their alliances solidified and their strategy in place, the Immortal Alliance was ready to take their first steps towards Olympus.

In the days leading up to their assault on Olympus, the Immortal Alliance focused on final preparations. Training intensified, with demigods and spirits alike honing their combat skills and mastering their abilities. Weapons and armor were forged and enchanted, ready for the battles to come.

Andrew, Kiara, Harry, and Adrian took time to reflect on their journey and the challenges that lay ahead. They knew that the path they had chosen was fraught with danger and uncertainty, but their resolve remained unshaken. They were united by a common goal, and their bond had grown stronger with each trial they faced.

One evening, as the sun set over the desolate landscape of Tartarus, Andrew gathered his companions for a final moment of reflection. They stood together at the edge of a cliff, overlooking the vast expanse of the abyss.

"We have come a long way," Andrew said, his voice filled with a mixture of pride and determination. "We have forged alliances, faced trials, and proven our worthiness. Now, we stand on the brink of war, ready to challenge the gods themselves."

Kiara placed a hand on Andrew's shoulder, her gaze steady. "Whatever happens, we face it together," she said. "We are stronger now than we have ever been, and we will not falter."

Harry and Adrian nodded in agreement, their expressions resolute. "We will fight for our freedom," Harry declared. "And we will show the gods that they are not invincible."

As the first stars appeared in the twilight sky, the Immortal Alliance stood together, their hearts filled with a sense of purpose and unity. They were ready to face the storm that was coming, and they knew that, whatever the outcome, they would face it as one.

The stage was set, the alliances were forged, and the strategy was in place. The Gathering Storm loomed on the horizon, and the Immortal Alliance was ready to unleash their fury upon Olympus. The time for preparation was over. The time for action had come.

Chapter 4

FORGING THE DARK ARMY

The first order of business was to train their diverse forces, molding them into a cohesive fighting force. The spirits of Erebus, the forces of the Underworld, the demigods of Camp Half-Blood, and now the mighty Titans—all brought unique strengths and abilities to the table. The challenge was to integrate these different groups into a unified army.

Andrew, Kiara, Harry, and Adrian, along with their advisors Chiron, Tartarus, Nyx, Chaos, and now Kronos, oversaw the training efforts. They established a massive training ground in the heart of Tartarus, a place where the different factions could come together and hone their skills.

Chiron took charge of the demigods and spirits, using his centuries of experience to teach them advanced combat techniques and battlefield strategies. His wisdom and patience were invaluable, helping to bridge the gap between the living and the dead, forging them into a single, cohesive unit.

"Focus on your strengths," Chiron instructed during a training session. "Demigods, use your divine heritage and unique abilities to your advantage. Spirits, harness the power of your ethereal forms to confound and outmaneuver your enemies."

The spirits of Erebus, with their ghostly forms and ability to move through shadows, proved to be exceptional scouts and spies. They trained in stealth and subterfuge, learning to blend into the darkness and strike from the shadows. Their ethereal nature allowed them to bypass physical barriers, making them invaluable in gathering intelligence and executing surprise attacks.

The forces of the Underworld, under the command of Hades, were relentless and disciplined. They trained in brutal close-quarters combat, their skeletal warriors and spectral hounds mastering the art of terror and intimidation. Hades himself oversaw their training, ensuring that his forces were prepared for the rigors of war.

"Fear is a weapon," Hades declared, his voice echoing through the training grounds. "Use it to your advantage. Let the enemies see their doom in your eyes and tremble before your might."

Kiara took on the role of tactical coordinator, working closely with Chiron and Hades to develop battle strategies that leveraged the strengths of their diverse army. She also focused on training the demigods in magical combat, teaching them to harness their innate abilities and channel their powers with precision and control.

Adrian, ever the inventor, worked tirelessly to create weapons and artifacts that would give their forces an edge in battle. His constructs, powered by his own unique abilities, ranged from enchanted weapons to defensive barriers, each designed to maximize their effectiveness in the upcoming conflict.

Adrian's workshop became a hub of innovation and creativity, a place where magic and technology merged to produce wonders of war. He drew inspiration from ancient myths and modern innovations, crafting weapons that could rival those of the gods themselves.

One of Adrian's first creations was a series of enchanted blades, forged from the darkest metals of the Underworld and imbued with the essence of Chaos. These blades were not only razor-sharp but also carried the power to disrupt magical barriers and weaken divine defenses. Each blade was unique, tailored to the strengths and abilities of its wielder.

"These weapons will cut through the lies of the gods," Adrian explained to the demigods and spirits. "Wield them with honor and determination, and no foe shall stand before you."

In addition to weapons, Adrian crafted powerful artifacts designed to protect and empower their forces. Shields that could repel divine magic, amulets that enhanced strength and speed, and cloaks that rendered the wearer invisible to mortal eyes—all were meticulously designed and enchanted to provide their army with every possible advantage.

One of Adrian's most ambitious projects was the creation of a massive, mobile fortress, a construct of iron and stone powered by the essence of Chaos. This fortress, known as the Obsidian Bastion, would serve as both a headquarters and a weapon, capable of moving across the battlefield and providing a formidable stronghold for their forces.

"The Obsidian Bastion will be the heart of our army," Adrian declared as he unveiled the towering construct. "It will shield us from our enemies and strike fear into their hearts."

With the weapons and artifacts complete, Adrian turned his attention to training the forces in their use. He held workshops and demonstrations, teaching the demigods and spirits how to wield the enchanted blades, activate the protective amulets, and harness the power of the Obsidian Bastion.

Realizing that their forces needed even more power to challenge Olympus, the Immortal Alliance set out to recruit Kronos and his Titans. Imprisoned in the depths of Tartarus, Kronos was a being of immense power and ancient knowledge. His hatred for the

Olympian gods ran deep, and Andrew believed that an alliance with the Titans could tip the scales in their favor.

Andrew, accompanied by Kiara, Harry, and Tartarus, ventured into the deepest recesses of Tartarus where Kronos and his Titans were bound. The air was thick with primordial energy, and the oppressive darkness seemed to pulse with latent power.

Kronos, bound by chains forged by Zeus himself, regarded them with eyes that burned with ancient fury. "Who dares to approach the King of the Titans?" his voice boomed, shaking the very foundations of Tartarus.

Andrew stepped forward, unflinching. "I am Andrew, chosen champion of Chaos and leader of the Immortal Alliance. We seek to overthrow the gods of Olympus and claim our rightful place. We need your strength, Kronos. Join us, and together we will bring down the tyrants who have imprisoned you."

Kronos's eyes narrowed, scrutinizing Andrew and his companions. "You speak of a grand ambition, mortal. What makes you think you can succeed where so many have failed?"

Tartarus, ever the loyal ally, spoke up. "The time of the Olympians is over, Kronos. Chaos herself has chosen Andrew. With your power and our combined forces, we can succeed."

Kronos considered this, his gaze shifting to Tartarus. "Very well. Release me from these chains, and I will lend my power to your cause. But know this, Andrew: the Titans will not be mere pawns in your game. We will have our revenge."

With Tartarus's help, Andrew and his companions broke the chains binding Kronos. As the ancient Titan rose to his full height, his power radiated through the abyss, a force of nature unleashed after millennia of imprisonment. The other Titans, sensing their leader's liberation, emerged from the shadows, their forms towering and imposing.

"Welcome to the Immortal Alliance," Andrew said, extending a hand to Kronos. "Together, we will bring Olympus to its knees."

Kronos grasped Andrew's hand, sealing their alliance. "Let the gods tremble. The Titans have returned."

The final test of their readiness came in the form of a skirmish with scouts from Olympus. Unbeknownst to the Immortal Alliance, Zeus and the other gods had grown suspicious of the activities in Tartarus and had sent scouts to gather intelligence and assess the threat.

The scouts, a group of elite warriors and spies, infiltrated the outskirts of the training grounds, hoping to gather information and report back to Olympus. However, the spirits of Erebus, ever vigilant, detected their presence and alerted Andrew and the others.

"Scouts from Olympus," one of the spirits reported, materializing before Andrew. "They seek to uncover our plans and weaken our resolve."

Andrew wasted no time. He summoned Kiara, Harry, Adrian, and Chiron, and together they formulated a plan to deal with the scouts. This would be their first true test, a chance to prove their readiness and send a message to Olympus.

"We must act swiftly and decisively," Andrew declared. "We cannot allow these scouts to report back to Olympus. Let this be a warning to the gods that we are prepared for whatever they send our way."

Kiara led a team of demigods and spirits to intercept the scouts, using her mastery of shadows to conceal their approach. Harry, with his brute strength and combat prowess, prepared for a direct confrontation, while Adrian set traps and defensive measures to corner and capture the scouts.

The skirmish began under the cover of darkness. Kiara and her team moved like wraiths through the shadows, surrounding the scouts and cutting off their escape routes. The scouts, realizing they had been detected, attempted to fight their way out, but they were met with a fierce and coordinated assault.

Harry led the charge, his enchanted blade cutting through the air with lethal precision. The scouts, though skilled and well-trained, were no match for the combined might of the demigods and spirits. They fought valiantly, but one by one, they fell to the relentless onslaught.

Adrian's traps activated as the scouts tried to flee, ensnaring them in webs of enchanted chains and binding them with magical restraints. The remaining scouts, realizing they were outmatched, surrendered, hoping for mercy.

Andrew approached the captured scouts, his gaze stern and unyielding. "Return to Olympus," he commanded. "Tell the gods that the Immortal Alliance is ready. We will not be cowed or defeated. Let them know that we are coming for them."

The scouts, their spirits broken, nodded in submission. They were released and sent back to Olympus with the message, a warning of the storm that was gathering in Tartarus.

The skirmish with the scouts proved to be a turning point for the Immortal Alliance. It demonstrated their readiness and unity, solidifying the bond between the different factions. The spirits of Erebus, the forces of the Underworld, and the demigods of Camp Half-Blood had fought together and emerged victorious, their resolve strengthened by the trial.

Andrew gathered the leaders of the alliance for a final meeting, a moment to reflect on their progress and prepare for the war ahead. They stood together in the grand hall of Tartarus, the map of the cosmos spread before them.

"We have faced many challenges," Andrew began, his voice filled with determination. "But we have overcome them through unity and strength. The gods of Olympus will not be defeated easily, but we are ready for whatever they throw at us."

Kiara, Harry, Adrian, and Chiron nodded in agreement, their expressions resolute. They had forged an army from the shadows and the depths of the Underworld, and they were prepared to challenge the might of Olympus.

Tartarus, Nyx, and Chaos, their ancient allies, watched with approval. They had seen the growth and determination of the Immortal Alliance, and they were confident in their ability to bring about the downfall of the gods.

"The time has come," Tartarus declared, his voice echoing through the hall. "The storm is upon us, and we must be ready to strike. Let Olympus tremble before the power of the Immortal Alliance."

As the leaders of the alliance stood together, their hearts filled with resolve, they knew that the war ahead would be long and difficult. But they were united in their purpose, ready to challenge the gods and claim their rightful place in the cosmos.

The dark army was forged, the alliances solidified, and the strategy in place. The time for preparation was over. The time for action had come.

Chapter 5

THE SIEGE OF OLYMPUS

The air above Olympus was thick with anticipation. The gods, once aloof in their ivory towers, now prepared for war. They had heard whispers of the Immortal Alliance's growing power, but they had underestimated the tenacity and unity of their enemies. Now, Andrew and his allies stood at the gates of Olympus, ready to unleash their fury.

Andrew, standing at the forefront, gazed upon the towering gates of Olympus. Behind him, the vast army of the Immortal Alliance stretched into the horizon. This army was a testament to their resolve and the alliances they had forged with Tartarus, Nyx, Chaos, and even the ancient Titans. Each warrior, each entity, had a burning desire for vengeance and freedom, united under the banner of Andrew's leadership.

"We fight not just for ourselves, but for the justice denied to us," Andrew declared, his voice echoing through the ranks. "Today, Olympus shall fall, and the gods will know the might of the Immortal Alliance!"

The gates of Olympus groaned open, and the defenders poured out, led by Ares, the god of war. His presence on the battlefield was a terrifying sight, his armor gleaming, and his spear crackling with divine energy. Zeus's thunderbolts split the sky, and Poseidon's trident called forth monstrous waves. The earth itself seemed to resist the advance of the Immortal Alliance, shifting and quaking under the influence of the gods.

Andrew raised his hand, signaling the charge. With a unified roar, the Immortal Alliance surged forward. Titans clashed with gods, primordial chaos met divine order, and the battlefield erupted into a frenzy of combat.

Kiara moved with the grace of a shadow, her daggers finding the gaps in the divine armor of the gods. Her every strike was lethal, her every movement calculated to sow confusion and disorder among the Olympian ranks. Harry, with his immense strength, was a force of nature, tearing through enemy lines with reckless abandon. His laughter was a terrifying contrast to the chaos around him.

Adrian, in the midst of the fray, wielded the artifacts he had crafted. His mechanical constructs, powered by both ancient and modern magic, roamed the battlefield, wreaking havoc on the Olympian forces. His inventions were a testament to his genius and a nightmare for his enemies.

The Titans, led by Kronos, were a sight to behold. Hyperion's flames scorched the heavens, while Atlas's immense strength and endurance provided a bulwark against the gods' mightiest attacks. Each Titan brought their unique power to bear, creating a formidable line that the Olympians struggled to breach.

Despite the overwhelming chaos, Andrew remained calm and focused. He knew that brute strength alone would not win this battle. They needed strategy, precision, and unyielding determination. Using his keen intellect, Andrew orchestrated a series of tactical maneuvers to outflank and outsmart the Olympians.

"Kiara, take your team and target the flanks. Disrupt their archers and mages," Andrew commanded, his eyes never leaving the battlefield. "Harry, hold the center with the Titans. Do not let them break our lines. Adrian, keep the constructs moving; we need to keep them guessing."

Kiara nodded, disappearing into the shadows with her team. They moved like ghosts, striking swiftly and silently, leaving chaos in their wake. The Olympian archers and mages found themselves under constant assault, unable to maintain their positions or provide support to their frontline troops.

Harry, with the support of the Titans, became an immovable force. He stood like a wall, deflecting attacks and delivering devastating blows in return. His laughter, mingled with the roars of the Titans, created a symphony of destruction that demoralized the Olympian forces.

Adrian's constructs were a constant source of confusion and frustration for the gods. They moved with uncanny agility, their attacks precise and relentless. Each construct was a masterpiece of engineering and magic, and Adrian commanded them with the precision of a maestro.

As the battle raged on, Andrew knew they needed a decisive moment to turn the tide in their favor. He spotted Zeus in the thick of the battle, his thunderbolts wreaking havoc among the ranks of the Immortal Alliance. Andrew knew that to break the spirit of the Olympian forces, they had to take down their king.

Gathering his strength, Andrew called upon the power of Chaos that coursed through his veins. With a determined expression, he advanced toward Zeus, his every step radiating power and confidence. The battlefield seemed to part before him as he made his way to the king of the gods.

"Zeus!" Andrew's voice boomed across the battlefield, capturing the attention of both allies and enemies. "Face me, if you dare!"

Zeus turned, his eyes blazing with fury. "You dare challenge me, mortal?" he roared, his voice shaking the very heavens. "I am the king of the gods, and you are nothing but a usurper!"

Andrew met Zeus's gaze with unwavering resolve. "I am more than a mortal," he declared. "I am the chosen of Chaos, and today, Olympus will fall!"

The two clashed with a force that shook the battlefield. Lightning met darkness, and the very air crackled with the intensity of their duel. Zeus's thunderbolts rained down upon Andrew, but he deflected them with his newfound power. Each strike was a test of their resolve, their will to dominate.

The battle between Andrew and Zeus was a spectacle of raw power and determination. Andrew drew upon the energy of Chaos, channeling it into his attacks. He felt the power surge through him, his strikes growing stronger, his resolve unbreakable.

Zeus, for all his divine might, found himself struggling to keep up with Andrew's relentless assault. The power of Chaos was unlike anything he had ever faced, its unpredictability and sheer force overwhelming his defenses.

But Zeus was not alone. The other Olympians rallied to his side, each bringing their unique powers to bear against Andrew and his allies. Hera's wrathful might, Poseidon's oceanic fury, and Athena's strategic brilliance combined to create a formidable opposition.

Andrew, sensing the shift in momentum, called out to his allies. "Hold the line! Do not let them break us!"

Just when it seemed that the Olympians might gain the upper hand, reinforcements arrived. Chiron, leading the forces of Camp Half-Blood, charged into the fray. The demigods, skilled in combat and fueled by their loyalty to Andrew, fought with unmatched ferocity.

"Fight on, for Andrew and the Immortal Alliance!" Chiron's voice rang out, rallying the demigods. Their arrival reinvigorated the Alliance, and the tide of battle began to turn once more.

The combined might of the Immortal Alliance and Camp Half-Blood was a sight to behold. They fought as one, their unity and determination driving them forward. The Olympians, despite their power, found themselves pushed back, their defenses crumbling under the relentless assault.

Despite the valiant efforts of the Immortal Alliance, the battle reached a critical point. Andrew realized that a prolonged engagement would only lead to unnecessary losses. With a heavy heart, he made a difficult decision.

"Fall back!" he commanded, his voice carrying over the din of battle. "Regroup and prepare for the next assault!"

The Immortal Alliance, though reluctant, followed Andrew's orders. They withdrew in an orderly fashion, their retreat covered by the Titans and the forces of Camp Half-Blood. The Olympians, battered and exhausted, did not pursue, their own forces in disarray.

As they regrouped, Andrew addressed his allies. "We have dealt a significant blow to Olympus today," he said, his voice steady. "But this battle is far from over. We must learn from this engagement, strengthen our forces, and prepare for the next assault."

Kiara, Harry, Adrian, and the other leaders nodded in agreement. They knew that this was but the first of many battles to come. The Siege of Olympus had tested their resolve and their unity, but it had also revealed their strengths and weaknesses.

"We will return," Andrew vowed, his eyes burning with determination. "And when we do, we will be stronger, wiser, and ready to claim our victory."

The Immortal Alliance, though temporarily set back, was far from defeated. They had shown their power, their unity, and their determination. The gods of Olympus now knew the true strength of their enemies, and the battle for the cosmos had only just begun.

Chapter 6

THE FALL OF A GOD

In the days following the Siege of Olympus, the Immortal Alliance regrouped in the depths of Tartarus. Despite the tactical retreat, spirits remained high. The battle had revealed their potential, but more importantly, it had shown that the gods were not invincible. Andrew knew they needed a significant victory to solidify their position and to prove to their allies and enemies alike that the Immortal Alliance was a force to be reckoned with.

Andrew, Kiara, Harry, Adrian, and their inner circle gathered around a large, ancient table carved from obsidian. Maps and scrolls were spread out before them, detailing the layout of Olympus and the positions of the gods.

"Our next target must be a decisive one," Andrew began, his gaze moving across his companions. "We need a victory that will shake Olympus to its core."

Kiara nodded, her eyes sharp. "Ares," she suggested. "The god of war. Defeating him would send a powerful message."

"Ares commands respect and fear among the gods and mortals alike," Adrian added, his mechanical hand tapping rhythmically on the table. "If we can defeat him, it will shatter the gods' morale."

Harry grinned, his muscles rippling with anticipation. "I've been itching for a rematch with him ever since our skirmish. Let's do it."

Andrew looked around the table, seeing the determination in the eyes of his friends. "It's decided then. We target Ares. But we need a plan, one that exploits his weaknesses and our strengths."

For days, the leaders of the Immortal Alliance devised their strategy. They knew that Ares would be expecting a direct assault, a show of brute force, which he would eagerly meet head-on. Instead, Andrew proposed a different approach: a combination of strategy, deception, and overwhelming power.

"We'll draw him out," Andrew explained, pointing to a valley near Olympus known for its ancient battlegrounds. "Ares won't be able to resist the lure of a fight on such sacred ground. But we'll control the battlefield, and we'll have surprises waiting for him."

Kiara and her team of assassins would create diversions, spreading misinformation about the Alliance's movements to confuse and mislead Ares. Meanwhile, Adrian would position his constructs and traps around the valley, ready to spring at the opportune moment.

Harry and the Titans would form the main force, ready to engage Ares directly. Andrew, wielding the power of Chaos, would be the linchpin, using his newfound abilities to turn the tide of battle at the critical moment.

The stage was set. Under the cover of darkness, Kiara and her team slipped into Olympus, spreading rumors and false intelligence about an impending attack on the heart of the gods' domain. The whispers reached Ares, who, true to his nature, could not resist the challenge.

"Andrew and his allies think they can take Olympus by storm," Ares growled, his eyes gleaming with anticipation. "Let them come. I'll crush them with my own hands."

As planned, Ares led his forces to the valley, a place where countless battles had been fought and legends had been born. The Immortal Alliance waited, hidden in the shadows, their traps set and their resolve unyielding.

The first light of dawn pierced the horizon as Ares and his warriors arrived in the valley. The god of war, clad in crimson armor and wielding a massive spear, exuded an aura of primal strength and ferocity. His soldiers, demigods and lesser deities, followed him with unwavering loyalty.

Andrew watched from a concealed vantage point, his eyes fixed on Ares. He could feel the power of Chaos coursing through him, ready to be unleashed. He signaled to Kiara, who nodded and vanished into the shadows.

With a sudden burst of movement, Kiara's team struck the first blow. Explosions rocked the valley as traps were triggered, sending plumes of smoke and debris into the air. Ares's forces were thrown into disarray, caught off guard by the unexpected assault.

"Now!" Andrew commanded, and the main force of the Immortal Alliance charged into the fray. Harry, leading the charge, roared a battle cry that echoed through the valley. The Titans followed, their immense forms crashing into the enemy ranks with devastating force.

Ares met Harry's charge with a savage grin. The two clashed, their blows shaking the ground beneath them. Harry's immense strength matched Ares's ferocity, their duel a whirlwind of steel and fury.

Around them, the battle raged. Adrian's constructs emerged from hidden positions, attacking Ares's soldiers with precision. Kiara moved through the chaos like a wraith, her daggers finding their marks with lethal efficiency.

Andrew watched, waiting for the right moment to strike. He knew that Ares would not fall easily, that it would take more than brute force to defeat the god of war. Drawing upon the power of Chaos, he prepared to tip the balance.

As the battle reached its peak, Ares began to push back Harry, his strength seemingly inexhaustible. Sensing the need for intervention, Andrew stepped forward, his eyes glowing with the dark energy of Chaos.

"Ares!" he shouted, drawing the god's attention. "Your reign of terror ends today!"

Ares turned, his eyes narrowing as he recognized Andrew. "You dare challenge me, boy?" he snarled. "I am the god of war! I will grind you into dust!"

Andrew raised his hand, and a wave of chaotic energy surged forward, engulfing Ares. The god of war staggered, caught off guard by the sheer force of the attack. Seizing the opportunity, Harry renewed his assault, driving Ares back.

Kiara and Adrian joined the fray, their coordinated attacks further weakening Ares. The god of war, for all his strength, found himself outmatched and outmaneuvered. The Immortal Alliance fought as one, their unity and strategy proving to be Ares's undoing.

With a final, desperate roar, Ares swung his spear at Andrew, who deftly dodged the attack and retaliated with a blast of chaotic energy. The force of the blast sent Ares crashing to the ground, his spear shattering upon impact.

Andrew stood over the fallen god, his gaze unwavering. "It's over, Ares," he said, his voice cold and resolute. "Your time has come."

Ares glared up at Andrew, defiance in his eyes. But he knew he was beaten. With a final, resigned growl, he collapsed, the light fading from his eyes.

The battlefield fell silent as the Immortal Alliance realized what they had accomplished. They had defeated a god, proving their strength and resolve. The impact of this victory would be felt across Olympus and beyond.

As the dust settled, Andrew and his companions surveyed the battlefield. The victory had come at a cost, but it was a significant step toward their ultimate goal. The fall of Ares would send shockwaves through the ranks of the gods, shaking their confidence and strengthening the resolve of the Immortal Alliance.

Andrew turned to his friends, his expression a mixture of pride and determination. "We've shown them what we are capable of," he said. "But this is only the beginning. We will continue to fight, to challenge the gods, until Olympus is ours."

Kiara, Harry, and Adrian nodded, their resolve unbroken. They knew that more battles lay ahead, that the path to victory would be long and arduous. But they also knew that together, they could achieve the impossible.

The defeat of Ares had a profound psychological impact on both the Immortal Alliance and the gods of Olympus. For the Alliance, it was a powerful validation of their cause, a tangible proof that they could stand against the might of the gods and emerge victorious.

For the Olympians, the fall of Ares was a stark reminder of their vulnerability. The gods, who had long considered themselves invincible, now faced a formidable and determined enemy. Fear and uncertainty began to creep into their ranks, their confidence shaken by the loss of one of their mightiest warriors.

In the days following the battle, Andrew and his allies worked tirelessly to strengthen their position. They fortified their defenses, trained their forces, and prepared for the inevitable retaliation from the gods. The victory over Ares had bolstered their ranks, with more entities and factions joining their cause, inspired by their success.

Andrew's leadership was instrumental in this process. He understood the importance of unity and morale, and he worked to ensure that every member of the Alliance felt valued and motivated.

He held strategy meetings, oversaw training sessions, and personally addressed any concerns or grievances.

Kiara, Harry, and Adrian also played crucial roles. Kiara's tactical acumen, Harry's unyielding strength, and Adrian's inventive genius complemented Andrew's leadership, creating a cohesive and effective command structure.

In Olympus, the mood was grim. The gods convened in the Hall of the Immortals, their expressions dark and their voices filled with anger and fear. Zeus, the king of the gods, stood at the head of the assembly, his eyes blazing with fury.

"We have underestimated them," Zeus admitted, his voice heavy with anger. "But we will not make that mistake again. We will regroup, strengthen our defenses, and crush this rebellion once and for all."

Hera, Athena, Poseidon, and the other gods nodded in agreement, their resolve hardening. They knew that they could not afford to be complacent, that the threat posed by the Immortal Alliance was real and growing.

The gods began to plan their counterattack, devising strategies to reclaim their dominance and restore their shattered confidence. They knew that the road ahead would be difficult, but they were determined to protect their realm and their power.

The fall of Ares marked a turning point in the conflict between the Immortal Alliance and the Olympian gods. It was a victory that resonated across the realms, a powerful statement of defiance and determination.

Andrew and his allies knew that there were many battles yet to be fought, that the struggle for supremacy would be long and arduous. But they also knew that they had the strength, the unity, and the resolve to face whatever challenges lay ahead.

As they prepared for the next phase of their campaign, they remained steadfast in their mission. The fall of a god was just the beginning. The Immortal Alliance was ready to continue their fight, to challenge the might of Olympus, and to forge a new destiny for themselves and the cosmos.

Chapter 7

TREACHERY WITHIN

In the aftermath of their victory over Ares, the Immortal Alliance basked in a fleeting moment of triumph. The fall of a powerful Olympian had bolstered their ranks, drawing new allies to their cause and deepening the commitment of those already with them. However, as the euphoria of their recent success began to fade, underlying tensions started to surface.

The diverse nature of the Alliance was both its greatest strength and its most significant vulnerability. The coalition included ancient entities from Tartarus, shadowy beings loyal to Nyx, chaotic forces of Chaos, and the disciplined warriors of Camp Half-Blood. While their shared goal of toppling Olympus unified them, centuries-old rivalries and mistrust simmered beneath the surface.

Kiara, ever watchful, was the first to notice the cracks forming within their ranks. In hushed conversations and secretive meetings, whispers of dissent and suspicion began to spread. She knew that if left unchecked, these seeds of discord could unravel everything they had fought for.

Andrew, sensing the growing unease, called a council meeting in the heart of Tartarus. The grand hall, carved from the living rock of the abyss, echoed with the murmurs of the gathered leaders. Andrew stood at the head of the table, his expression serious and resolute.

"We have achieved a great victory," he began, his voice carrying the weight of authority. "But we cannot afford to become complacent. The gods are regrouping, and we must remain united if we are to stand against them."

Tartarus, Nyx, and Chaos themselves attended, their forms imposing and enigmatic. Representatives from Camp Half-Blood, including Chiron, sat alongside the Titans and various other factions. The atmosphere was tense, with old grudges and new alliances clashing silently.

"United?" A voice rang out from the end of the table, dripping with skepticism. It was Althea, a powerful demigoddess from Camp Half-Blood. "How can we trust beings who have spent millennia plotting against us? How do we know they won't betray us at the first opportunity?"

Murmurs of agreement spread through the hall. Andrew raised a hand, calling for silence. "Trust must be earned," he said firmly. "And I believe we have taken the first steps in that direction. But we must also be vigilant. We cannot allow suspicion to divide us."

Despite Andrew's efforts, the seeds of distrust continued to grow. Adrian, ever the inventor, had been working on new weapons and defenses, spending long hours in his forge. His absences, though innocent, were twisted by rumors into something more sinister.

"He's building something to destroy us," one of the Titans muttered to Kiara. "He's always been too close to the Olympians for my liking."

Kiara, loyal and sharp-eyed, decided to investigate. She confronted Adrian in his workshop, the heat of the forge casting flickering shadows on the walls. "Adrian, you need to be more transparent," she urged. "People are starting to question your loyalty."

Adrian looked up from his work, his expression weary. "I'm doing what I can to give us an edge," he replied. "But I understand. I'll make an effort to communicate more."

As Kiara and Adrian worked to quell the rumors, a darker plot began to unfold. Unbeknownst to Andrew and his inner circle, a faction within the Alliance had begun to conspire against him. This group, led by a disgruntled former ally named Lysander, believed that Andrew's leadership was leading them to ruin.

Lysander, a powerful sorcerer from the depths of Nyx's domain, had grown increasingly resentful of Andrew's prominence. He saw the young leader as a usurper, someone unworthy of the power and respect he commanded. Gathering a small but influential group of dissidents, Lysander began to plot Andrew's downfall.

"We cannot let a mortal, no matter how powerful, dictate our fate," Lysander hissed to his followers. "Andrew must be removed, and the Alliance restructured under true leadership."

Kiara, ever vigilant, sensed something amiss. Her instincts led her to the darker corners of Tartarus, where she overheard whispers of betrayal. Following the threads of the conspiracy, she uncovered Lysander's plot and realized the imminent danger to Andrew and the Alliance.

Without wasting a moment, Kiara rushed to Andrew's quarters, finding him deep in strategic discussions with Harry and Adrian. "Andrew, we have a problem," she said urgently, outlining the conspiracy.

Andrew listened intently, his expression darkening with each word. "We need to act swiftly," he said. "But we must also handle this delicately. We cannot let this divide us further."

That night, under the cloak of darkness, Andrew and his closest allies moved to confront Lysander and his conspirators. They found them in a secluded chamber, plotting their next move.

"Lysander," Andrew called out, his voice echoing through the chamber. "We need to talk."

Lysander and his followers turned, shock and defiance in their eyes. "Andrew," Lysander sneered. "I should have known you'd catch on. But it's too late. Your time as leader is over."

Andrew stepped forward, his demeanor calm but resolute. "Why, Lysander? Why betray us now, when we need unity the most?"

"Because you are leading us to destruction!" Lysander spat. "You are a mortal playing at being a god. You do not understand the forces you are dealing with."

Andrew took a deep breath, steadying himself. "I may be mortal, but I have the support of Tartarus, Nyx, and Chaos. We have accomplished great things together. This is not about me; it's about all of us."

As the confrontation escalated, it became clear that this was not just about Lysander's jealousy. It was a test of Andrew's leadership and his ability to unite a fractured alliance. He knew that brute force alone would not resolve this; he needed to appeal to the underlying grievances and fears.

"Listen to me," Andrew implored, addressing both Lysander and his followers. "I understand your concerns. The path we are on is perilous, and I do not claim to have all the answers. But we have come too far to let mistrust tear us apart. We must stand together, or we will surely fall."

There was a tense silence as Lysander's followers hesitated, uncertainty flickering in their eyes. Andrew's words had struck a chord, revealing the depth of their shared fears and hopes.

Kiara stepped forward, her voice firm and reassuring. "Andrew has proven himself time and again. He has brought us victories and shown us that the gods are not invincible. We must give him our trust, not our suspicion."

In that pivotal moment, Lysander's resolve began to waver. The presence of Tartarus, Nyx, and Chaos themselves, watching from the shadows, lent weight to Andrew's plea for unity.

Lysander finally lowered his head, acknowledging his defeat. "Perhaps I was wrong," he admitted, his voice tinged with regret. "Perhaps we can find strength in unity after all."

Andrew stepped forward, placing a hand on Lysander's shoulder. "We need you, Lysander. Your power and knowledge are invaluable. Let us move forward together, as one."

With the conspiracy unveiled and defused, the Alliance began to heal. The experience had tested their unity and resolve, but it had also strengthened their bonds. The internal conflict had served as a harsh but necessary lesson: only by trusting and supporting one another could they hope to achieve their goals.

In the days that followed, Andrew worked tirelessly to restore trust within the Alliance. He held open forums, encouraging dialogue and addressing concerns. He ensured that every faction felt heard and valued, fostering a sense of camaraderie and mutual respect.

Kiara, Harry, Adrian, and the other leaders supported him, reinforcing the message of unity and cooperation. The threat of betrayal had been a wake-up call, reminding them all of the delicate balance they needed to maintain.

The gods of Olympus, meanwhile, watched from their lofty perch, unaware of the internal struggles their enemies had faced. They remained focused on their preparations, oblivious to the renewed strength and determination of the Immortal Alliance.

As the Alliance regrouped and prepared for the next phase of their campaign, they did so with a renewed sense of purpose. The betrayal had been thwarted, their unity tested and affirmed. They knew that more challenges lay ahead, but they also knew that they were stronger together.

Andrew stood before his assembled allies, his voice filled with conviction. "We have faced our own demons and emerged stronger for it. Let this be a reminder that our greatest strength lies in our unity. Together, we will achieve the impossible."

The hall erupted in a chorus of cheers and applause, the sound echoing through the depths of Tartarus. The Immortal Alliance was ready to face whatever challenges lay ahead, united and resolute in their quest to reshape the cosmos.

Chapter 8

THE POWER OF PROPHECY

The recent internal strife within the Immortal Alliance had underscored the importance of unity and trust. Now, with their bonds reaffirmed, Andrew and his companions turned their attention to the next critical phase of their quest: seeking the Oracle of Delphi. The ancient seer held the key to unlocking deeper insights into their destiny and preparing them for the final confrontation with the gods of Olympus.

As the Alliance gathered to embark on their journey, Andrew addressed them with a determined resolve. "The prophecy has guided us thus far, but we need to uncover its full meaning to ensure our success. The Oracle of Delphi will provide the clarity we need."

The journey to Delphi was fraught with peril. The path led through treacherous terrains, mystical forests, and territories still under the influence of the Olympian gods. Each step was a test of their endurance, unity, and resolve.

The first trial came as they traversed the enchanted Forest of Illusions, a place where reality warped and twisted, reflecting the deepest fears and desires of those who entered. The forest's magic was designed to disorient and divide, preying on the weaknesses of the travelers.

Andrew and his companions entered the forest cautiously, the air thick with an eerie mist. Shadows danced at the edge of their vision, and whispers filled the air, sowing seeds of doubt and fear.

Kiara, ever vigilant, took the lead, her keen senses guiding them through the maze of illusions.

"Stay close and focus on each other," she instructed. "The forest will try to separate us, but we must remain united."

Despite their best efforts, the illusions took their toll. Adrian was haunted by visions of his past failures, while Harry saw glimpses of a future where their quest ended in ruin. Even Andrew, with his unwavering determination, was not immune. He saw a vision of himself standing alone on a desolate battlefield, his allies fallen around him.

Drawing strength from each other, they pressed on, using their bond to navigate the forest's deceptions. With Kiara's guidance and Andrew's leadership, they finally emerged from the Forest of Illusions, their unity stronger than ever.

As they neared Delphi, the Alliance faced another formidable challenge: the Guardians of Delphi. These ancient protectors were tasked with ensuring that only the worthy could access the Oracle. Each guardian represented a different element and virtue, testing the travelers in unique ways.

The first guardian, a towering figure made of stone and earth, challenged them to a test of strength and endurance. Adrian, with his powerful artifacts, stepped forward, using his creations to withstand the guardian's might and earn their passage.

The second guardian, a being of fire and fury, demanded a test of courage. Harry, known for his bravery, faced the flames unflinchingly, proving his mettle and securing their way forward.

The third guardian, a spirit of water and wisdom, posed a riddle that required both intelligence and insight. Kiara, with her sharp mind and strategic acumen, solved the riddle, allowing them to proceed.

Finally, the fourth guardian, an ethereal presence of air and truth, required a test of honesty and integrity. Andrew, embodying these virtues, spoke of their quest, their struggles, and their determination to reshape the world. His sincerity and conviction convinced the guardian to grant them access to the Oracle.

With the guardians' trials behind them, the Alliance entered the sacred chamber of the Oracle of Delphi. The air was thick with ancient magic, and the presence of the seer was palpable. The Oracle, an ageless figure shrouded in mystery, awaited them on a raised dais.

"Welcome, seekers of truth," the Oracle intoned, her voice resonating with power. "You have come to learn your destiny and uncover the path that lies ahead."

Andrew stepped forward, bowing respectfully. "We seek guidance, great Oracle. We need to understand the prophecy that has brought us this far."

The Oracle's eyes glowed with an otherworldly light as she began to recite the prophecy from the second book:

"In the shadows' grasp, the claimer shall rise, Their grip unyielding, dominion in their eyes. Olympus shall falter, its glory laid to rest, As the new dawn yields to the Darkblade's test."

The chamber fell silent as the weight of the words settled over them. The Oracle continued, her voice filled with ancient wisdom and foreboding.

"Andrew, you are the claimer, destined to rise from the shadows and challenge the might of Olympus. Your journey has been fraught with trials, but you have proven your strength and resolve. The Darkblade, a weapon of immense power, will be the key to your victory. But be warned: with great power comes great responsibility. The path ahead is perilous, and the choices you make will shape the fate of all realms."

Andrew listened intently, the gravity of the revelation sinking in. He knew that the prophecy held both promise and peril, and that the Darkblade would be a double-edged sword, capable of bringing both salvation and destruction.

Armed with the Oracle's insights, the Alliance began their preparations for the final confrontation with the gods of Olympus. Andrew and his companions spent days in intense training, honing their skills and mastering their newfound powers. They forged new strategies, combining their strengths and abilities to create a formidable force.

Adrian worked tirelessly in his forge, crafting powerful weapons and artifacts imbued with the essence of Tartarus, Nyx, and Chaos. Harry, Kiara, and the warriors of Camp Half-Blood trained rigorously, pushing themselves to their limits to be ready for the battles to come.

Andrew, bearing the weight of his destiny, focused on mastering the Darkblade. The weapon responded to his will, its power resonating with his own. He knew that the final battle would test him in ways he had never imagined, and he needed to be prepared for anything.

As the days turned into weeks, the Alliance grew stronger and more united. They were no longer just a group of allies; they were a family, bound by their shared quest and the trials they had faced together.

On the eve of their departure for Olympus, the Alliance gathered for one last meeting. The atmosphere was charged with anticipation and resolve. Andrew stood before them, his presence commanding and inspiring.

"We have come a long way," he began, his voice steady and confident. "We have faced countless challenges and emerged stronger for it. The prophecy has guided us, and now we stand on the brink of our final confrontation. Remember what we fight for: a new dawn, a world free from the tyranny of the gods. Together, we will achieve the impossible."

The hall erupted in a chorus of cheers and applause, the sound echoing through the chamber. The Alliance was ready, their spirits unbroken and their resolve unwavering.

As they prepared to leave Delphi, the Oracle's final words lingered in Andrew's mind. The path ahead was fraught with danger, but he knew that they were ready. They had the strength, the unity, and the prophecy to guide them.

With the dawn of a new day, the Immortal Alliance set out on their final journey. The power of prophecy had revealed their destiny, and they were determined to see it through to the end. The gods of Olympus awaited, but the Alliance was ready. The stage was set for the ultimate battle, and the fate of the cosmos hung in the balance.

Chapter 9

THE BATTLE OF TITANS

The air was charged with palpable tension as the Immortal Alliance made their final preparations. They stood on the brink of Olympus, the heart of their enemy's power. The path to the peak was steep and treacherous, guarded by formidable defenses and the ever-watchful eyes of the gods. Andrew, bearing the weight of leadership and destiny, led the charge.

"We stand at the threshold of our destiny," he proclaimed, his voice steady and resolute. "Today, we fight not just for ourselves, but for a future free from tyranny. Olympus will fall, and a new era will begin."

His words were met with a chorus of determined voices, a resounding echo of their collective resolve. The Immortal Alliance, a coalition of gods, demigods, titans, and mortal heroes, was united under a common banner. They had trained tirelessly, forged powerful alliances, and gathered an army capable of challenging the very heavens.

Andrew cast a glance at his closest companions: Kiara, her eyes blazing with determination; Harry, his grip on his weapon firm and unwavering; and Adrian, who had forged weapons and artifacts of immense power. Each of them had faced their own trials and emerged stronger, their bonds unbreakable.

As they began their ascent, the ground beneath them trembled with anticipation. The path to Olympus was fraught with danger, but they were undeterred. Tartarus, Nyx, Chaos, and the spirits of the dead marched alongside them, a formidable force that shook the very foundations of the world.

The ascent was not without its challenges. As they climbed higher, they encountered the first line of defense: a battalion of celestial warriors, clad in gleaming armor and wielding weapons that glowed with divine light. These warriors, the loyal protectors of Olympus, were ready to defend their realm with their lives.

Andrew raised his hand, signaling the Alliance to halt. "Prepare for battle," he commanded, his voice carrying over the ranks. "We face the guardians of Olympus. Show no fear, for we are stronger together."

The battle erupted with a deafening clash of steel. Andrew, wielding his sword imbued with the power of Chaos, led the charge. He moved with a grace and precision that belied his mortal origins, cutting through the ranks of celestial warriors with ease. Kiara fought at his side, her mastery of elemental magic turning the battlefield into a tempest of fire and lightning.

Harry and Adrian, each wielding weapons of their own creation, engaged the enemy with equal ferocity. Harry's sword, a blade forged in the fires of Tartarus, cleaved through divine armor as if it were mere cloth. Adrian's staff, imbued with the essence of Nyx, cast shadows that ensnared and disoriented their foes.

The celestial warriors fought valiantly, but they were no match for the combined might of the Immortal Alliance. One by one, they fell, their divine essence dissipating into the ether. As the last of the defenders were vanquished, the Alliance pressed onward, their resolve unshaken.

The path led them to the gates of Olympus, massive structures of gold and marble that gleamed in the sunlight. Beyond the gates lay the city of the gods, a realm of unparalleled beauty and power. But for the Immortal Alliance, it was a place of tyranny and oppression, a symbol of the gods' unchecked dominion.

Andrew stood before the gates, his hand resting on the hilt of his sword. "We are here," he declared, his voice echoing off the walls of the city. "Open the gates and face us, or we shall bring them down."

For a moment, there was silence. Then, with a creaking groan, the gates began to open. Standing at the threshold was a figure clad in golden armor, a god whose presence radiated power and authority. It was Athena, the goddess of wisdom and war, her eyes burning with a fierce determination.

"You dare to challenge the gods?" Athena's voice was both a command and a warning, resonating with the power of ages.

Andrew stepped forward, his gaze unyielding. "We seek justice," he replied. "And we shall have it, no matter the cost."

With a nod from Athena, the gates swung open wider, revealing the assembled forces of Olympus. The Olympian gods had gathered, their combined power a formidable barrier against the advancing army. Zeus, Poseidon, Hera, and the other major gods stood ready, their faces set in grim determination.

The battle for Olympus was a sight to behold, a symphony of chaos and destruction. The gods, once thought invincible, found themselves on the defensive. The Immortal Alliance, driven by their desire for justice and freedom, fought with a ferocity that matched the gods' own.

Andrew and Athena clashed with a fury that shook the heavens. Each strike of their weapons sent shockwaves through the battlefield, and the ground cracked and splintered beneath their feet. Athena fought with the power of a god, her every movement a testament to her divine strength and wisdom. But Andrew, with the power of Chaos coursing through him, matched her blow for blow.

Around them, the battle raged on. Kiara faced off against Poseidon, the god of the sea. Their duel was a clash of elemental forces, each trying to outmaneuver the other. Poseidon, with his control over water, launched powerful waves and torrents, but Kiara's mastery over fire and earth gave her an edge, turning the battlefield into a chaotic storm.

Harry found himself pitted against Apollo, the god of the sun. The radiant light of Apollo's arrows clashed with the dark energy of Harry's sword, creating a dazzling display of light and shadow. Despite Apollo's divine power, Harry's determination and skill allowed him to hold his ground, each strike bringing him closer to victory.

Adrian, wielding his staff of shadows, took on Hermes, the messenger god. Hermes' speed and agility were unmatched, but Adrian's control over darkness allowed him to anticipate and counter Hermes' attacks. Their duel was a dance of shadows and light, each trying to outwit the other.

The battle raged on, the air filled with the sounds of clashing weapons and the cries of the wounded. The gods, once confident in their supremacy, began to falter under the relentless assault of the Immortal Alliance. The tide of battle was turning, but the cost was high.

As the battle reached its peak, Andrew saw an opportunity to weaken the gods' defenses. He called out to his allies, his voice cutting through the chaos. "We need to break their ranks! Focus your attacks on their weakest points!"

The Alliance responded with a coordinated assault. Tartarus unleashed a horde of shadowy creatures that swarmed the battlefield, sowing confusion and panic among the gods' forces. Nyx enveloped the area in darkness, blinding their enemies and giving the Alliance an advantage.

Chaos, ever unpredictable, summoned a storm of raw energy that tore through the gods' defenses. The very fabric of reality seemed to warp and twist under her influence, creating chaos that the gods struggled to contain.

With their forces in disarray, the gods found themselves on the defensive. Andrew seized the moment, pressing the attack with renewed vigor. He fought with a determination born of desperation and hope, each strike bringing him closer to victory.

Athena, battered and bloodied, finally fell to Andrew's blade. The goddess of wisdom and war, a symbol of Olympus' might, lay defeated at his feet. The sight of their fallen comrade sent a ripple of fear through the gods' ranks, their confidence shattered.

But the battle was far from over. The gods, driven by their own pride and desperation, rallied their forces for a final stand. Zeus himself, the king of the gods, descended from his throne, his presence radiating power and authority.

"You have fought bravely," Zeus declared, his voice booming across the battlefield. "But your rebellion ends here. I will show you the true power of the gods."

The final confrontation was a battle of titanic proportions, the forces of the Immortal Alliance pitted against the full might of Zeus. The ground shook with the impact of their blows, and the air crackled with the energy of their magic.

Andrew faced Zeus with a determination that belied his mortal origins. He knew that this battle would determine the fate of their rebellion, and he fought with every ounce of strength he possessed. His sword, imbued with the power of Chaos, clashed with Zeus' thunderbolts, creating a dazzling display of light and energy.

Kiara, Harry, and Adrian fought alongside him, their combined powers a match for the king of the gods. They moved as one, their attacks coordinated and precise, each strike bringing them closer to victory.

Zeus, for all his power, found himself on the defensive. The Immortal Alliance, driven by their desire for justice and freedom, fought with a ferocity that matched his own. The tide of battle was turning, but the cost was high.

As the battle raged on, Andrew saw an opportunity to weaken Zeus' defenses. He called out to his allies, his voice cutting through the chaos. "Focus your attacks on his weak points! We can bring him down!"

The Alliance responded with a coordinated assault. Tartarus unleashed a horde of shadowy creatures that swarmed the battlefield, sowing confusion and panic among Zeus' forces. Nyx enveloped the area in darkness, blinding their enemies and giving the Alliance an advantage.

Chaos, ever unpredictable, summoned a storm of raw energy that tore through Zeus' defenses. The very fabric of reality seemed to warp and twist under her influence, creating chaos that Zeus struggled to contain.

With their forces in disarray, the gods found themselves on the defensive. Andrew seized the moment, pressing the attack with renewed vigor. He fought with a determination born of desperation and hope, each strike bringing him closer to victory.

The battle for Olympus was reaching its climax. The Immortal Alliance had pushed the gods to their limits, but the cost was immense. As the fighting continued, the toll of the conflict became evident. Lives were lost, and the cries of the wounded filled the air.

In the midst of the chaos, Kiara, Harry, and Adrian found themselves facing insurmountable odds. The gods, driven by desperation, launched a fierce counterattack. Kiara, using her elemental magic, created a barrier of fire and ice to protect her comrades. Harry and Adrian fought valiantly, their weapons clashing against divine forces.

But even their combined strength was not enough. As a powerful wave of energy surged towards them, Kiara made a split-second decision. She pushed Harry and Adrian out of harm's way, taking the full brunt of the attack herself. The force of the blast knocked her to the ground, her body battered and broken.

"Kiara!" Harry's voice was filled with anguish as he rushed to her side. Adrian, his eyes wide with horror, followed close behind.

Kiara's breath came in ragged gasps. "It's... it's okay," she whispered, her voice barely audible. "You have to keep fighting. For all of us."

Harry and Adrian nodded, their eyes filled with determination and grief. They rose to their feet, their resolve stronger than ever. With renewed vigor, they launched themselves back into the fray, their attacks fueled by the memory of their fallen comrade.

As the battle raged on, Andrew found himself locked in a fierce duel with Zeus. The king of the gods fought with a ferocity born of desperation, his thunderbolts clashing against Andrew's blade of Chaos. The ground trembled with each strike, and the air crackled with the energy of their conflict.

"Your rebellion ends here!" Zeus roared, his voice echoing across the battlefield. "You are no match for the power of the gods!"

Andrew's grip tightened on his sword. "We fight for justice and freedom," he replied, his voice steady and unwavering. "We fight for a future where tyranny has no place."

With a roar of fury, Zeus launched a powerful attack, a bolt of lightning that tore through the air towards Andrew. But before it could strike, a figure stepped between them. It was Harry, his sword raised to deflect the attack. The lightning struck the blade, dispersing into the air with a deafening crack.

"Not today," Harry said, his voice filled with determination. "We won't let you win."

Zeus' eyes narrowed with anger. "You dare to defy me?"

Harry's grip on his sword tightened. "We dare."

With a coordinated assault, Andrew and Harry pressed the attack. Their combined strength and determination drove Zeus back, each strike weakening his defenses. The tide of battle was turning, and for the first time, the king of the gods looked uncertain.

As the battle reached its climax, Zeus unleashed his full power, a storm of energy that shook the very foundations of Olympus. The ground cracked and splintered, and the air was filled with the deafening roar of thunder.

But the Immortal Alliance stood firm. Andrew, Harry, Adrian, and their allies fought with a determination that matched the gods' own. They moved as one, their attacks coordinated and precise, each strike bringing them closer to victory.

With a final, desperate effort, Zeus launched a powerful attack, a bolt of lightning that tore through the air towards Andrew. But before it could strike, Chaos intervened. Summoning a storm of raw energy, she deflected the attack, creating a shield that protected the Alliance.

"You will not win," Chaos declared, her voice filled with an otherworldly power. "The era of the gods is over."

With a roar of fury, Zeus launched himself at Chaos, their powers clashing in a dazzling display of light and energy. The ground trembled with the impact of their blows, and the air crackled with the energy of their conflict.

But even the king of the gods was no match for the combined might of the Immortal Alliance. With a final, coordinated assault, they drove Zeus to his knees. His thunderbolts dissipated into the air, and his power waned.

Andrew stepped forward, his sword raised. "It's over," he said, his voice steady and resolute. "The reign of the gods has come to an end."

With a final strike, Andrew brought his sword down, the blade of Chaos cutting through the divine essence of Zeus. The king of the gods fell, his body dissolving into the ether.

The battle was over. The ground was littered with the fallen, and the air was filled with the echoes of their final cries. The Immortal Alliance had emerged victorious, but the cost had been high. Lives had been lost, and the scars of battle would linger for years to come.

As the sun began to set, casting a golden light over the battlefield, Andrew stood amidst the ruins of Olympus. His sword, still glowing with the power of Chaos, was sheathed at his side. He looked out over the city, a realm of unparalleled beauty and power, now a symbol of their hard-won freedom.

Amidst the devastation, a glimmer of hope remained. Kiara lay on the ground, her body battered and broken, but she was alive. Harry and Adrian rushed to her side, their faces etched with concern and determination.

"Kiara, stay with us," Harry pleaded, his voice choked with emotion.

Adrian knelt beside her, his hands glowing with the faint light of healing magic. "We'll get you through this," he said, his voice steady despite the fear in his eyes.

Andrew approached, his heart heavy with the weight of their sacrifices. He knelt beside Kiara, placing his hand on her forehead. "Hold on, Kiara," he whispered. "We've come too far to lose you now."

Summoning the power of Chaos within him, Andrew channeled it into a healing force. His hand glowed with a radiant light as he poured his energy into Kiara's broken body. Slowly, her wounds began to mend, the cuts and bruises fading away. Her breathing steadied, and her eyes fluttered open.

"Andrew..." Kiara's voice was weak but filled with gratitude. "Thank you."

Andrew smiled, relief flooding his heart. "We need you, Kiara. We all do."

With Kiara stabilized, the Immortal Alliance began to regroup. The gods' reign had ended, but their journey was far from over. They had a new world to build, a future to create.

As the sun dipped below the horizon, casting the battlefield in a serene twilight, Andrew stood with his closest allies. Harry and Adrian stood beside him, their faces reflecting a mixture of exhaustion and determination. Kiara, now able to stand with their support, looked out over the ruins of Olympus with a resolve that matched their own.

"We did it," Harry said, his voice filled with a mix of relief and hope. "We actually did it."

Andrew nodded, his gaze unwavering. "We did. But the fight isn't over. We have to rebuild, to create a world where tyranny has no place."

Adrian's eyes glowed with determination. "We will. For everyone who fought and for the future we're fighting for."

As the Immortal Alliance began to organize their next steps, Andrew took a deep breath. The battle for Olympus had been won, but their journey was just beginning. They had a new world to build, a legacy to forge.

With a final glance at the ruins of Olympus, Andrew turned to his comrades. "Let's get to work," he said, his voice filled with quiet resolve. "Our journey is just beginning."

And with that, the Immortal Alliance set out to forge a new destiny, their hearts filled with hope and determination. The gods had fallen, but the dawn of a new era had just begun.

Chapter 10

A NEW DAWN

The dawn broke over a transformed Olympus, the golden rays of the sun illuminating the remnants of the epic battle that had reshaped the very fabric of the cosmos. The once-proud city of the gods now stood as a testament to the Immortal Alliance's victory, a symbol of the dawn of a new era.

As the dust settled, the battlefield was a scene of both triumph and sorrow. The fallen lay where they had fought, their sacrifice etched into the annals of history. Among the ruins, the surviving members of the Immortal Alliance began to regroup and assess the cost of their hard-won victory.

Andrew, now imbued with the power of Chaos and the mantle of leadership, stood at the heart of the devastation. His eyes, glowing with the energy of his new powers, surveyed the scene with a mixture of resolve and sorrow. Kiara, badly injured but alive, lay nearby. Andrew knelt beside her, his hands glowing with a soft, healing light as he channeled his power to mend her wounds.

"You did it, Andrew," Kiara whispered, her voice weak but filled with pride. "You led us to victory."

Andrew smiled gently, his eyes filled with gratitude. "We did it, Kiara. Together."

With a final surge of energy, Andrew closed Kiara's wounds, and she sighed in relief, strength returning to her limbs. He helped her to her feet, and together they turned to face their allies.

The surviving Olympian gods, their pride and power broken, approached Andrew with a mixture of fear and resignation. Hera, Demeter, Hermes, and the other remaining gods knelt before him, their once-proud forms humbled by the defeat of their king and the fall of Olympus.

"Andrew," Hera spoke, her voice trembling but dignified. "We acknowledge your victory. Olympus is yours."

Andrew regarded them with a steady gaze, the weight of his new responsibilities pressing upon him. "Rise," he commanded. "Olympus will not be ruled by fear or oppression. We will rebuild it, together."

The gods rose, a mixture of relief and uncertainty in their eyes. Andrew's words were a promise of a new beginning, one where justice and power would be balanced.

A grand ceremony was held amidst the ruins of the great hall of Olympus. The gods and members of the Immortal Alliance gathered to witness Andrew's coronation. Tartarus, Nyx, and Chaos stood by his side, their presence a testament to the new order that had risen from the ashes of the old.

Adrian, Harry, and Kiara watched with pride as Andrew ascended to the throne, the crown of Olympus placed upon his head. The air was thick with anticipation, the cosmos holding its breath as Andrew spoke his first words as the new ruler.

"Today marks the beginning of a new era," Andrew declared, his voice resonating with power and authority. "An era where justice, freedom, and unity shall reign. We will rebuild this world, not as rulers and subjects, but as allies and equals."

The crowd erupted in cheers, the promise of a brighter future igniting hope in their hearts.

With his allies by his side, Andrew began the monumental task of rebuilding the cosmos. He divided the territories among his trusted friends and the remaining gods, each given dominion over different aspects of the new world.

As the ruler of Olympus and the cosmos, Andrew retained the central power, overseeing the overall governance and ensuring balance among the territories. He took dominion over the realm of the heavens, maintaining the cosmic order.

Recognized for her bravery and strength, Kiara was named the Goddess of the Sun. She was given dominion over the solar realm, her light serving as a beacon of hope and renewal for the cosmos.

With his skill in crafting powerful artifacts, Adrian became the God of Forge and Creation. He took charge of the realm of industry and craftsmanship, responsible for building and shaping the new world.

Known for his wisdom and strategic mind, Harry was appointed the God of Knowledge and Diplomacy. He governed the realm of intellect and communication, serving as a guide and counselor to all.

Given his role in the Alliance and his ancient power, Tartarus retained dominion over the abyss and the darker aspects of the cosmos, ensuring the balance of light and darkness.

As the primordial deity of night, Nyx was given control over the realm of the night, her powers maintaining the balance between day and night.

As the primordial force of creation and destruction, Chaos maintained influence over the elemental forces and the void, ensuring the fundamental balance of the cosmos.

The former king of the Titans, Kronos was granted dominion over the temporal realm, his powers governing time and its passage.

The remaining Olympian gods were given roles and territories aligned with their domains. Hera took charge of the realm of marriage and family, Demeter the realm of agriculture and harvest,

Hermes the realm of trade and communication, and others were assigned territories fitting their powers and responsibilities.

The wise centaur and mentor, Chiron, was granted dominion over the realm of healing and education, his wisdom guiding the development and well-being of the inhabitants of the new world.

With the territories divided and the new order established, Andrew turned his attention to reconciliation. He reached out to former enemies, offering them a place in the new world. Many accepted, their hearts moved by Andrew's vision of unity and justice.

The integration of these former enemies brought new strengths and perspectives to the Immortal Alliance, their combined efforts ensuring the stability and prosperity of the new order.

As the days turned into weeks and the weeks into months, Andrew and his allies reflected on their journey. They had faced unimaginable challenges, their bonds tested and strengthened by the trials they had endured. Together, they had forged a new path, their legacy one of unity, justice, and power.

Andrew stood on the balcony of the rebuilt palace, looking out over the transformed Olympus. Beside him, Kiara, Adrian, and Harry stood, their presence a reminder of the strength and courage that had brought them to this moment.

"We've come a long way," Kiara said, her voice filled with wonder.

"Indeed we have," Adrian agreed. "And we've only just begun."

Andrew smiled, his heart filled with hope and determination. "The future is ours to shape," he said. "Together, we will ensure that this new dawn brings light and prosperity to all."

And so, under the leadership of Andrew and his allies, the cosmos entered a new era. An era of balance, justice, and unity, where the legacy of the Immortal Alliance would endure for generations to come.

Chapter 11

THE EMPIRE OF GOLD

The once chaotic and tumultuous cosmos had given way to a serene and structured empire, now known as the Empire of Gold. Andrew's reign marked a period of unparalleled prosperity, justice, and unity, drawing inspiration from the values and principles that had guided the Immortal Alliance through their arduous journey.

Upon securing his position as the ruler of Olympus and the cosmos, Andrew's first task was to establish a system of laws and governance that would ensure fairness, justice, and the well-being of all inhabitants. This new order required a meticulous approach, as it aimed to integrate the diverse territories and their unique cultures under a unified banner.

Andrew formed the Council of Realms, an assembly comprising representatives from each of the newly established territories. The council included Kiara as the Goddess of the Sun, Adrian as the God of Forge and Creation, Harry as the God of Knowledge and Diplomacy, Tartarus overseeing the abyss, Nyx governing the realm of night, Chaos as the custodian of elemental forces and the void, Kronos as the Titan of Time, Hera as the Goddess of Marriage and Family, Demeter as the Goddess of Agriculture and Harvest, Hermes as the God of Trade and Communication, and Chiron as the Lord of Healing and Education.

The Council met regularly to discuss matters of state, propose new laws, and resolve disputes. This democratic approach ensured that all voices were heard and that governance was a collaborative effort.

Andrew, with input from the Council, drafted the Codex of Unity, a comprehensive set of laws that outlined the rights and responsibilities of all citizens, the governance structure, and the principles of justice and equality. The Codex emphasized equality, justice, unity, sustainability, and innovation. All beings, regardless of origin, were granted equal rights and opportunities. A fair judicial system was established to resolve conflicts and ensure justice. The Codex encouraged collaboration and understanding among diverse cultures, protected and preserved the environment and natural resources, and promoted advancements in knowledge, technology, and arts.

The war had left deep scars, and Andrew understood the importance of reconciliation to heal these wounds and build a stable future. He embarked on a series of initiatives aimed at reconciling with former enemies and integrating their followers into the new order.

Andrew extended an olive branch to the surviving forces of Olympus who had opposed him. He offered them amnesty and a place in the new order, provided they swore loyalty to the Codex of Unity. Many accepted this offer, their desire for peace and stability outweighing past grievances.

The Concord of Peace was formalized in a grand ceremony where former enemies publicly swore allegiance to Andrew and the new order. This act of reconciliation was a powerful symbol of unity and a commitment to a shared future.

To facilitate the integration of former enemies and their followers, Andrew established various programs aimed at promoting understanding, cooperation, and unity. These included cultural exchange programs, encouraging the sharing of customs, traditions, and knowledge among different territories; education initiatives, providing education and training to all citizens, with a focus on the values of the new order; and community building projects, joint projects aimed at rebuilding and enhancing communities, fostering a sense of shared purpose and belonging.

Recognizing the emotional and psychological toll of the war, Chiron, as the Lord of Healing and Education, spearheaded efforts to provide healing and support to those affected. Healing centers were established across the territories, offering physical and mental health services.

As the Empire of Gold flourished, Andrew and his allies often reflected on the journey that had brought them to this point. The path had been fraught with challenges, but it had also forged unbreakable bonds and instilled invaluable lessons.

Each member of the Immortal Alliance had grown in their own way. Andrew's journey from a mortal leader to the ruler of the cosmos had been marked by immense personal growth. He had learned the importance of compassion, justice, and the balance of power.

Kiara, as the Goddess of the Sun, had embraced her role as a beacon of hope and renewal, her light guiding the new era. Adrian's craftsmanship and creativity had flourished, leading to innovations that benefited all.

Harry's wisdom and strategic mind had been instrumental in navigating the complexities of governance and diplomacy.

Tartarus's understanding of the balance between light and darkness had ensured the stability of the new order.

Nyx's role as the custodian of the night had deepened, her presence a reminder of the importance of rest and reflection.

Chaos's influence over the elemental forces had brought a sense of balance and harmony to the cosmos.

Kronos's control over time had ensured that the past was honored, and the future was planned with care.

The legacy of the Immortal Alliance was etched into the very fabric of the Empire of Gold. Their journey had been one of sacrifice, courage, and unwavering resolve. They had faced insurmountable odds and emerged victorious, their unity and determination creating a new era of peace and prosperity.

Monuments and memorials were erected across the territories, honoring the heroes and their sacrifices. The stories of their journey were taught in schools, ensuring that future generations understood the values and principles that had shaped their world.

As they looked to the future, Andrew and his allies remained committed to their vision of a just, fair, and united cosmos. They continued to work tirelessly to address new challenges and seize new opportunities, their leadership guiding the Empire of Gold towards a bright and prosperous future.

The Solar Realm, under Kiara's guidance, transformed into a vibrant and dynamic hub of energy and light. The solar realm became the center of technological advancements, with solar energy powering much of the Empire of Gold. Kiara's influence extended to agriculture, where innovative farming techniques ensured abundant harvests. The solar realm also became a cultural center, hosting festivals and celebrations that drew visitors from across the cosmos. Kiara's light was a symbol of hope and renewal, her presence a constant reminder of the warmth and vitality that sustained life.

Adrian's realm, the Forge of Creation, was a testament to the power of creativity and innovation. The Forge of Creation was a bustling center of industry and craftsmanship, where artisans and inventors from across the cosmos came to collaborate and create. The forge produced not only powerful artifacts and weapons but also everyday items that improved the quality of life for all citizens. Adrian's leadership encouraged experimentation and exploration, leading to breakthroughs in various fields, from engineering to the arts. The Forge of Creation became a symbol of progress and ingenuity, its influence felt in every corner of the empire.

Harry's realm, the Library of Knowledge, became the intellectual heart of the empire. Housing vast collections of books, scrolls, and artifacts, the library was a place of learning and discovery. Scholars from all territories came to study and share their knowledge, fostering a culture of continuous learning and intellectual growth. Harry's diplomatic skills ensured that the library remained a neutral ground, where ideas could be exchanged freely, and conflicts could be resolved through dialogue and understanding.

Tartarus and Nyx, guardians of the abyss and the night, maintained the balance between light and darkness. Their realms were places of contemplation and reflection, where individuals could find solace and inner peace. Tartarus's deep understanding of the duality of existence helped maintain stability, while Nyx's gentle presence reminded all of the importance of rest and introspection. Together, they ensured that the empire remained harmonious and balanced, embracing both the light of day and the calm of night.

Chaos, as the custodian of elemental forces and the void, brought a sense of balance and harmony to the empire. His influence was felt in the natural world, where the elements were in perfect equilibrium. Chaos's realm was a place of raw power and untamed beauty, a testament to the primordial forces that underpinned the cosmos. His presence reminded all of the importance of respecting nature and living in harmony with the environment.

Kronos, the Titan of Time, oversaw the temporal realm. His control over time ensured that the past was honored, and the future was planned with care. The temporal realm was a place of reflection and foresight, where individuals could learn from history and prepare for the future. Kronos's wisdom and patience guided the empire, ensuring that decisions were made with a deep understanding of their long-term consequences.

Hera, Demeter, and Hermes played vital roles in maintaining the social and economic fabric of the empire. Hera, as the Goddess of Marriage and Family, promoted unity and harmony within families and communities. Her influence ensured that relationships were nurtured and that the bonds of love and kinship remained strong. Demeter, as the Goddess of Agriculture and Harvest, ensured that the land remained fertile and that there was abundance for all. Her realm was a place of growth and renewal, where the cycles of nature were respected and celebrated. Hermes, as the God of Trade and Communication, facilitated the flow of goods and information across the empire. His realm was a bustling hub of activity, where trade routes connected distant territories and where ideas and innovations could spread quickly.

Chiron, as the Lord of Healing and Education, played a crucial role in the well-being of the empire's citizens. Healing centers and schools were established across the territories, offering physical and mental health services and providing education and training to all. Chiron's realm was a place of learning and healing, where individuals could seek knowledge and find solace. His influence ensured that the empire remained healthy and that its citizens were well-informed and capable.

As the Empire of Gold continued to flourish, Andrew and his allies looked to the future with hope and determination. They remained committed to their vision of a just, fair, and united cosmos, their leadership guiding the empire towards a bright and prosperous future.

The journey had been long and challenging, but it had forged unbreakable bonds and instilled invaluable lessons. The legacy of the Immortal Alliance was etched into the very fabric of the Empire of Gold, their story a testament to the power of unity, courage, and unwavering resolve.

Andrew stood on the balcony of his palace, gazing out over the bustling city below. The sun was setting, casting a golden glow over the landscape. He felt a sense of peace and fulfillment, knowing that their efforts had brought about a new era of peace and prosperity.

Kiara joined him, her presence warm and comforting. She took his hand, and together they watched as the sun dipped below the horizon, ushering in the night.

"We've come a long way," Kiara said softly, her eyes reflecting the last rays of sunlight.

"Yes, we have," Andrew replied, his voice filled with gratitude and determination. "And we have much more to do. But for now, let's take a moment to appreciate all that we've achieved."

The stars began to twinkle in the sky, their light a reminder of the vastness and beauty of the cosmos. Andrew and Kiara stood together, their hearts filled with hope and their spirits unwavering.

The Empire of Gold was a beacon of unity and prosperity, a testament to the power of collaboration and the strength of the human spirit. And as the stars shone brightly overhead, Andrew knew that their journey was far from over. The future was theirs to shape, and together, they would continue to build a world where justice, peace, and harmony reigned supreme.

The End.

Don't miss out!

Visit the website below and you can sign up to receive emails whenever Tharun Vigneswar PS publishes a new book. There's no charge and no obligation.

https://books2read.com/r/B-A-LBUIB-NWJJD

BOOKS2READ

Connecting independent readers to independent writers.